This book belongs to

the fabulous, *wonderful*,

MOST EXCELLENT

Ana

This book is dedicated to everyone in Walberswick,
where we spend every Christmas – R. CURTIS

For Finn and Mia – R. COBB

PUFFIN BOOKS
UK | USA | Canada | Ireland | Australia | India | New Zealand | South Africa
Puffin Books is part of the Penguin Random House group of companies
whose addresses can be found at global.penguinrandomhouse.com.

www.penguin.co.uk   www.puffin.co.uk   www.ladybird.co.uk

Penguin
Random House
UK

First published 2020
This paperback edition published 2021
001
Text copyright © Richard Curtis, 2020
Illustrations copyright © Rebecca Cobb, 2020
The moral right of the author and illustrator has been asserted
Made and printed in China
A CIP catalogue record for this book is available from the British Library
ISBN: 978–0–241–39361–1

Imported into the EEA by Penguin Random House Ireland,
Morrison Chambers, 32 Nassau Street, Dublin D02 YH68

THAT
Christmas

Written by
Richard Curtis

Illustrated by
Rebecca Cobb

PUFFIN

On the East coast there's a village
and in that village lived five families.

This is what we looked like . . .

Our parents had all been friends for years – and all of us children
had been friends basically since we were babies.

In the winter we spent every cold and wet day in each other's houses –
and in the summer we spent every sunny day on the ▆▆▆▆▆

Every year, we always spent Christmas Day
with each other in a big barn,
where we had *quite* a lot of

There were **The Presents** –

there was **The Lunch**,
turkey and ALL
the trimmings –

there was
The Washing-Up . . .

There was **The Big Walk** –

~~there was Visiting the Neighbours~~

there was Watching Christmas TV

and then we went To Bed.

Same thing every year – just as GOOD every year – but *always* the same.

But then what happened That Christmas happened.

It was when we were nine – that's us, Scarlett and Spike.
And for the rest of our lives, **we all never, ever forgot it**.

This is WHY it happened – two days before Christmas,
all our parents went away because some friends
were getting married on an island nearby.

And because Bernadette had just turned sixteen, they agreed that just for one night we could all sleep together without a babysitter. And they'd get back on Christmas Eve.

But the next day, just as our parents were about to leave the island, a terrible storm broke out – and the boat that was going to bring them back simply couldn't sail because the people in it would have been tossed into the sea and died.

So suddenly there were ~~NO GROWN-UPS LEFT TO TAKE CARE OF US ON CHRISTMAS DAY.~~

Our parents managed to contact us – and they gave us a huge list of exactly what we should do for every minute of Christmas Day and we all promised we would do everything exactly as they said.

But what they didn't realize was . . .

. . . we all had our fingers crossed.

So began what would forever after be called . . .

Because – even though children absolutely LOVE Christmas – it is a very important life lesson that everything can always be improved.

So, we made some little changes.

First, obviously, **The Presents**.

Everyone knows that adults are only *quite* good at presents because they always give presents they *wish* their children would play with, but children know they won't.

So, the older children peeked at all the presents on Christmas Eve –
and then swapped the presents that were a bit TOO serious
for ones that were a bit more FUN.

Right there and then,
Christmas was already
23 per cent better.

Next we sorted out **The Lunch**.

Christmas food is all very well and awfully nice for parents to make
the things that remind them of when they were young and Queen Victoria
was Queen – but everyone knows that they could do a lot better.

So we chose good stuff and had the BEST Christmas lunch ever
with LOTS of decent modern food
and NO Brussels sprouts.

yes

Christmas improved
by 26 per cent.

Us two also found an original way of doing **The Washing-Up**,
which was usually the WORST part of Christmas Day.

Instead it was very nearly the BEST.

Next up, we all put on our coats and hats and scarves and boots
for **The Big Walk**.

We weren't going to miss that — though we did *slightly* change the route.
Much, much shorter and **100 per cent** better.

We also didn't forget to **Visit the Neighbours**.
Though this year, we did a lot more than
just have a boring cup of tea with the
remarkable Miss Timkins.

The next thing to sort out was **Watching Christmas TV**.

NO speech by the Queen, NO movie made in the last century in black and white, NOTHING with anything to do with hymns or vicars or people being especially Christmassy nice to each other.

A proper viewing schedule was worked out.

On lots and LOTS of different
screens, of course.

Improvement **17 per cent**.

Finally, we did get a bit tired . . .

But then, just before the lights went out, Bernadette remembered
something her Granny told her a long time ago. She said "*shush*" –
and this was the last thing we heard that night . . .

"*But let's not forget – in the middle of all the fun –*"

And we all cheered because
we *had* had LOTS of fun.

"Yes indeed. But don't forget who started it. You see, Christmas is the actual birthday of this amazing baby and when he was born some completely **AMAZING** kings, with actual **BIG** beards, came and gave him completely amazing presents, including some actual **GOLD**.

And the incredible thing is that this baby – who as far as I remember was born basically in a barn – grew up to be a really extraordinary person. And he said really wonderful things, like that

we should be **kind** to each other,

and **love** each other,

and NOT *fight*.

And this really rings a bell with people all over the world –
no matter where they live and what they believe in.

And that's why we're all here together tonight – because we actually
love each other and on Christmas Day we really **know** it.

And **show** *it.*"

And then we all dozed off together in the barn.

Then first thing in the morning something quite good happened.
Our parents caught a really early boat and came home.
And although they were rather surprised
by the sight that met their eyes . . .

. . . they were really, REALLY happy to see us.

And when they asked us how it had gone,
we said it had been *lovely* and we'd done
everything ALMOST *exactly* the same.
But of course it hadn't been *quite* as
good without them there.

What they didn't see was that, once again,
our fingers were *just a little bit* crossed.

The **next year**, everything went back to **normal** —
and we were all as happy as cupcakes.

But secretly, we knew
we had *already* had our

BEST

Christmas *ever*.

So *this* Christmas we strongly suggest that you ask if you can maybe –
just maybe, perhaps, **please** – have, well, a *little* bit of . . .

THAT
Christmas
too.

The End